T0077531

# On the Road

# to

# Damascus

by

Dr. Patrick T. Dougherty

&

published by

❋Wayward Bride Press❋

in cooperation with Trafford Publishing

Order this book online at www.trafford.com
or email orders@trafford.com

Most Trafford titles are also available at major online book retailers.

© Copyright 2004 Dr. Patrick T. Dougherty.
All rights reserved. No part of this publication may be reproduced, stored in a retrieval system, or transmitted, in any form or by
any means, electronic, mechanical, photocopying, recording, or otherwise, without the written prior permission of the author.

Print information available on the last page.

ISBN: 978-1-4120-2254-5 (sc)
ISBN: 978-1-4122-2162-7 (e)

Because of the dynamic nature of the Internet, any web addresses or links contained in this book may have changed
since publication and may no longer be valid. The views expressed in this work are solely those of the author and do
not necessarily reflect the views of the publisher, and the publisher hereby disclaims any responsibility for them.

Any people depicted in stock imagery provided by Getty Images are models, and
such images are being used for illustrative purposes only.
Certain stock imagery © Getty Images.

*Trafford rev. 12/02/2020*

 www.trafford.com

**North America & international**
toll-free: 844-688-6899 (USA & Canada)
fax: 812 355 4082

For
Aya, Jasmine and Clio --
the angels in my life.

# A note from the author:

The first clash of my idealism with the reality of the streets came in my third week of teaching when I learned the sound that bullets make when they ching against brick and cement.  I had finished a day of classes and the kids had been good.  I was feeling satisfied that I was reaching more than a few of them there, in old room 210, in my ragged school south of the highway in Phoenix, Arizona.

I had gotten a glass of water from the cooler in the office and was walking to the social studies supply room to get some drawing paper for an assignment that I was creating for the next day.  I was walking along the side of the liberal arts building near the street when the gunfire erupted.

Iconographic images played out before me.  A young man dressed in white jeans and a white tank top was running, a silver car sizzled to a halt behind him, two young men in sunglasses flew from the gut of the car and pulled guns . . . the young man twenty feet from me, the two men in pursuit, running, running towards me, and then flashes and sound.  Blood on the tank top and on the jeans, the two men disappearing from view as I focused on the fallen image on the sidewalk.  I felt water on my hand and realized that I was shaking.

# Oveture:

# On Teaching

You forever feel

immured

transfixed

to the shore


Its mystical in doses

harsh and brittle in pieces

like cuts of glass falling

through water by degrees


Like a builder of ships

you saw

cut

weld

hammer

tear apart

rebuild

curse and sweat


Then all you can do

*is stand on the shore and wave*

*as the creations wrought from your toil*

*slip their coils*

*take sail*

*and disappear*

---

# Act One

# I

entr'acte

# AMY: A POEM IN TORN PIECES

# On the Road to

# Damascus

*Prima luce...*

*half past five in the morning...*

Crimson light paints the wall where I saw the gecko rest last night, answering my gaze with amethyst eyes, watching  me as the radiance of the dying sun wove a coppered halo that fired the horizon, sketching in Chinese brushstrokes the jagged crista of mountains that filed on toward the west and California.

My thoughts tug me from beneath the waves of sleep and summon me to breach the surface of my reverie; yet, I lay and float on the still-pond surface of dreams.  My wife's doe soft breathing and the enveloping energy of dawn are the only companions for my thoughts.

I think of Egypt.  Ancient dawns ascending the tombs in the Valley of Kings.  Karnak, Luxor, splendid graves, tombs of silver, onyx and ivory, golden masks that stare across centuries demanding obeisance. Tides of sand that come to shore about the pyramid monuments of god-kings. Ra, Ramses, and the tale of Moses.  Sphinx riddles and scarab beetles, the pounce of eons dancing in the spear shafts of light, ravishing the dusk of centuries. Regeneration and immortality.  Immortal covenants.  Isis and a fugue of transcendence.

Deserts, Sumer, Babylon, Gilgamesh, blue robed bedouins, camels sailing the sands, Arabia, the thousand and one nights . . . Coffee.

I slide away from the amber warmth of my wife's body,
stand and let the dizziness float from my brain.
Rubbing my eyes, I entice my  blood to flow again.  I
glide through the room, letting the mossy rings of
stupor slide from my thoughts.  The bathroom light hits
like a fist at my eyes.  I see the image in the mirror.
The crease of a pillow shows on the stranger's face I
see peering back -- a Byzantine saint, stiff, bearded,
pale, and impossible of mirth.

The morning calmness sits like a presence in the silence
of my rooms.  I pull on my robe and walk through its
cobwebbed essence to my door and the paper, wrapped and
neat, innocent looking for the news it keeps.  A child
with a grenade.  Buried in its pages is the world beyond
the monastic walls of my life.

One cup, two, three, the bitter tang sharpening my
senses.  Headlines.  Gays Parade.  Palestinian Suicide
Bombers.  Israeli Cabinet Debates.  I search for the
comics.

I stand, stretching, creaking my ribs toward the
ceiling.  In the hazy mountains of West Virginia a pool
of Elizabethan English gathers in the forest hollows.
The cragged ones still name the body with a rough term--

"The Bone Box."  I think of Shakespeare's dust.  Then I notice the loose sheets of paper on the counter.  The poem.  Kanji-like words drifting free on the yellow paper; I decipher a few words from my scribbled hieroglyphs:


*In Memory of  Bernice . . .*


I look at the time, corral the sheets in my battered briefcase and begin my ascent.

[AMY, A FOURTEEN-YEAR-OLD STUDENT,

A FRESHMAN,

RAN AWAY FROM HOME --

WE NEVER SAW HER AGAIN]

Traffic glints in my mirrors , and the primal angle of the sun hits the rearview with daggers.  Phoenix is hot cement and steel.   I hurtle along, following the ant trail of traffic up a corridor sliced in the desert. Late September and the temperature still hovers near 100.   Back home, where I grew up, on the eastern shore of Lake Michigan, autumn is in the air, the leaves are starting to drain of emerald and take on their gold and amber hues, but not here, not in the Valley of the Sun. My price for bougainvilleas in December, a few months of hell.  I see the brown haze over the western horizon-- an aerial flourish for the city of fallen angles, decadent, nihilistic, exporting its smog to the desert...the breath of perdition . . . roaches will inherit the earth.

National Public Radio splashes out its litany . . . words, names, places, ideas, dreams, and nightmares . . . Afghanistan, Somalia, Iraq, Yemen, on and on  . . . they rollick like bats on the waves of air.

Regions, shatter-spirited, were the devil prances a tarantella amid horrific misery...plagues...the Dance of Death, Durer wood blocks, the Four Horsemen, Apocalypse. Medieval tombs . . .  silent effigies squirm grotesque. Images of putrefaction, worms coil in eye sockets, bloated toads emerging from the relics of ribs.  Old

Nick laughs among the embers.

# III

I spit words of

fire in my heart

The office rests in twilight, and a secretary sits captured like an icon in an efflorescent platinum halo thrown from her desk lamp.  Dark Ages, candles burning on the rough hewn desks, ancient clerics scribble the names of God in desperation of the darkness that panther slithers and circles them, panting with bloodied breath horrors from oblivion, the unknown, shadows beyond the walls, Basilisks twirl in the far hills, and all huddle frightened against the death dripping fangs of the night.

No epistles from the office.  A note from a counselor -- a wayward student, the face comes to mind as I stroll out onto the quad and toward my building.  And, ah, there, leaning against the construction fence.  Jorge. Jorge of the counselor note.  Piss driven.  He says he hates school, but always he is here-- were else to go in this neighborhood unless you risk death in the parks or tread among the broken glass and syringes in the alleys. So many.  Our sentinels of the early and late hours.  A reality that shimmers beneath the heart movements of teachers during the crucifixion of sixth hour, before the bell sounds across the dry courtyards, before the squirming larva grow legs and crash into the corridors eager to flee, but stay.  No wings for true flight, dusk finds them by the vending machines, waiting out the sinister blackness of broken windows before the leviathan night closes them in her gut.

# IV

burn the

temples of my

thoughts

I go to my room, old 210, noticing how desiccated the grass seems, parched and sizzled.  Deserts. The Gobi. Sahara, Kalahari, Taklamakan sands, reg, rocky shores on the oceans of sand, the singing hills of far Asia, tales of  Saint-Exupery, a haunted calling of the azan... lands of prophets and of madmen.

I click the door and let in Raul.  Raul the Wanderer. He comes into being with each dawn, reborn to stand by my paint-chipped door. Raul the lanky hermit, the poet-haired one immersed again in a novel of magic and kingdoms of ether, where dragons argue ideology with gnomes and are both slain with laser points --story lines that the captains of the Enterprise warping through space would welcome as home.

He glides to a desk, back corner on the right, the same as yesterday, and shall the same be tomorrow -- constants.  The  sunrise, the sunset, the full moon, and Raul.

I splash out the remnant grounds of coffee from my cup out onto the parched grass.   Three girls call gum snapping greetings as they flounce by, laughing and buzzing, flaunting the dress code with bare midriffs and skin hugging micro minis.  The desert attire of stardusted teenage hearts on the prowl.  They  sneak

*XVIII*

each morning into gas station restrooms to metamorphose,

paint on make-up, tug on miniskirts, and dangle jewelry

-- fruits forbidden by Mexican fathers, harsh fathers,

who as young men worshiped the girls who snuck into

washrooms to emerge like new butterflies in the morning

sun.

# V

with anger

raged across

wild memories

I walk back into the room, enter the cave, looking for
the truth beyond the shadows.

My desk sits, a leaden lump, vintage military and old,
perhaps, as the globe that was the sole adornment when I
inherited this abode of learning.  My House of Wisdom.
My Sorbonne.  Ah, the globe.  On its yellowed vision of
Earth, with its red pen marks and sea swirls rest images
of countries that exist no longer; yet, I hold it still
for to toss it away would be to forsake a senile aunt.

Past teachers who walked this faded carpet include one
who left to die in Africa.   Far away places, dreams on
the Serengeti, the shadow of Kilimanjaro, lions panting
beyond the campfire.  Eidetic images.  Great Zimbabwe,
Mansa Musa, the gold of the Sudan, Zanzibar . . .

From my desk I take my briefcase and remove its
contents.  An archaeologist dissecting a mummy.  Pens,
slips of memos, papers, and the poem.  I glance at it,
remembering.  Its words bubble images into my brain.

*When you hear the wind, call her name*
    *and ask if she remembers me*

The first bell rings, I hear the legions stir, moving
voices, a battle commencing.  And, as if distant

*XXI*

thunder, my mind echoes the clash of ancient swords.

# VI

cast ember

burning to the

tinder

buttresses

"Ladies and Gentlemen, we've been studying ancient Egypt, let's review a few cogent points before tomorrow's test."

The sand cascades into the opening, ripped from the earth, a caesarean in time, centuries buried beneath the soft treading of sandals, beneath the beggar's bowl rested the fortune of ages.  The tomb sparkles as if filled with fireflies, a lantern I hold and peer into the heart of eternity.

I have searched each dwelling, torch in hand and mourning on; yet, no mustard seed do I uncover; no breath of life to resurrect this death I have known. Questions as unanswerable as the riddles in a bee's dream assail my senses deep below the level of words. Perhaps on an unattainable plateau a clue rests, guarded by enigmas too profound to even view. The speculation of Olympian truths belongs in the  realm of gods. Where is our Prometheus now, to yield us another comfort?

# VII

of my

wandering

mind

Two people, now three, there in the back of the room whisper soft as dove wings on misted air. Margie came in, tears welling in her almond eyes... rubies.  Plaster saints staring, crucifixion bound, votives flashing echoes of life in the pupils of their painted eyes.

Love crushed in flower, the usual... and again we go against the antinomians.   I ignore the quiet chatter, I let her Antigones assuage her pain...unfold again the wings, golden against the breeze, and cast thyself forth onto sapphrine skies, to skate above the orange and ovening day. Ancient of days  be merciful  and heal.

# VIII

# An inhabitant of a smaller universe

The bell sounds its cacophony wail.  The students resurrect, electric and charging, banging, out into the brilliant radiance of the sun.

"Remember the test! Force yourselves, study!"

In the distant regions of my memory, I hear the conch sound, calling in the darkness, above the black waters in the night.

I walk back to my desk, savoring the moment's peace, brief as a moth's wing against a flame.  I pick up the paper and decipher again the lines of my poem...

"Hi Dr. D.!"
"Maestro!  We are here!"

The tang of armor and sword, cries of anguish and triumph echoing from the palisade cliffs, blood mingles with tears, and the sands drink up the ebbing lives as they stream from broken bodies. I imagine scintillating souls pirouetting in the smoke above the now silent battlefield.

# IX

I fumble

about its

constellations

Three hours, ninety souls, I shepherd in I shepherd out.
Bequeathed to me by an office as mysterious as a Druidic
priest. Decisions made on the casting of bones. Yet,
here they find their way. Pilgrims in a life so little
their own. I am a way station, an oak under whose boughs
they rest, sheltered by the gathering leaves. So I like
to think and dwell to keep from easy anguish my heart.
With these myths I anoint my inner being with oil,
consecrate and absolve with the fire of violet skies
under which I seek my truths.  Echoes I hear unchained
in the valley, splashing up mountains in their passion
to escape.

# X

briefly join in

the timeless

minuet

Homeroom. Attendance and silence. Reading time. Quiet. I
feel the sopor of death receding slowly, as a mist will
retreat before the rising sun. And I meditate again on
where my thoughts dwelt this night last.  And why.

I follow the gold thread back and come again before the
silent face encircled by roses.  The weeping summons
itself to my mind's ear.  I climb the ascent, it's seven
levels acquiesce before me.  I can hear the pianissimo
coo of doves.

# XI

## of an orbit

## here then

## there

The bell.

Smashing sounds as books are hurled back onto straining shelves.

Noon.  Lunch.  Respite.  My loyal mendicants appear at the door.  They enter as they always do.  The same students every day.  Timeless.  Continuous. They pull themselves into my harbor once again, to take the air that will get them through the  tattered remnants of the day.

I answer questions, offer some time to their thoughts. Till the garden, entice the lotus to breach the algaed surface and bloom.  Writing my legacy in blood upon each soul.  Finally, I cease my benedictions and place my heart back in its reliquary.

Then I retreat, as they watch CNN on the class T.V., to my desk, and the sheaf of papers within which lies the skeleton of my emotion from last night.  I shift my grade book, and find the words.

It's on its own now, an entity fashioned from the clay of my thoughts.  Evanescence caught in ink and born to the page, caged like a peregrine, breaking its wings against the walls of its cell.

*XXXIV*

# XII

among the

orbs that

skate the

heavens

Again the bell.  The noon wanderers depart.  Silence reigns in the room.  Velvet quiet.  My prep hour.  I open my grade book, turn on my computer, and begin to set down marks.  Neat vertical rows of numbers.  Hours of effort boiled down to simple figures.  Life.  Death and the obituaries.  A whole life enshelled in the space of a paragraph.  So transient . . . the chatter that sounds like chimes.

# XIII

and soon I

leave or am

forced away

I ache a bit with the morning's efforts.  That dryness I taste, the subtle cricking in my legs and along the snake line of my spine . . . here come the pilgrims, the murmur of prayer, the chant weaving itself through the incense misted nave.  I hear a canticle being sung. Again my children, we begin.  I know the acclivity of morning is past, and downward slopes the day to the vastness of the desert afternoon.

"Remembering that you have a test tomorrow, I thought it'd be a good idea to review some main points."

Egypt and the shade of pyramids . . . sweat hewn and back broke mountains of transcendence . . .  Death was a gossamer veil to god-kings.

Death has grown, from myriad gods we beg deliverance. Kali stalks the imagination, gurgling for throats to slit out there, beyond the chalky shores of consciousness.  Night-horrors, enclosing tombs, the fodder of worms.

# XIV

## to crash with

## comet haste

The final hour.  I walk to the board and erase a few comments that I will write again in a few moments pace.

My mind floats on the stream of time, clicking seconds pull me forward, and the adagio kaleidoscope view of the bank adjusts with each minute.  My daydreams soar far above it all, my thoughts cloak themselves in pilgrim guise and search through centuries and the crevices of eras, floating and eddying on time's river, so dark and purple deep as it glides above its bedrock of bones.  I chant a mantra to the stars as I float beneath their diamond gaze and hear their antiphon aerial murmur in the beating of my heart.  All so soft, as a child's breath in sleep on a summer afternoon . . .

# XV

## to new

## directions

## reaching still

The bell sounds, I set my marker down with its fellows,
in the green can by the file cabinet, the crowd responds
to my wave and crashes like hell-bent stallions through
the door.

Emptied in a second, the room stands quiet and formal as
I walk bone weary back to my desk.  I lift the sheet
with its poem, hold it to the light and read.

A few hours later, past the meetings, phone calls, and
grading, I step out of the room, turn and close the
door, hear the metal click of the lock, and begin my
walk to the parking lot.  The harsh sun has mellowed
into a red ball of fire, igniting the clouds and gilding
the peripheral sky.  The mountains are vermillion
slashes against the white and gold of the horizon.

I think of a statement I scribbled once on the back of a
memo, standing at the office counter as the day end
chaos whirled about me and mailbox doors snapped open
and shut.  I don't know where the lines came from.
Their origins were like a muse whisper, unexpected and
compelling, and so I jotted down the words with the snub
of a very old pencil:

*His mind ceased to comprehend,*

*but his heart began to know.*

# XVI

always for the

gentle halo tug

of a gravity that

fits my own

# On the Road to Damascus
Dr. Patrick T. Dougherty

*In memory of  my student*

*in memory of Bernice . . .*


*When you hear the wind, call her name*

*and ask if she remembers me . . .*


*Sweat and perfume were entwined*

*tastes twirled in the dust that settled and rose from the naked yard . . .*

*I stepped from among the low-slung cars and the amber twilight*

*and  joined the muted crowd's movement inward*

*to the cinder block church*

*tiny and chipped yellow*

*cast among the weary homes in the lazaret neighborhood*

*there below the bridge*


*Her classmates were gathering*

*timid to view the shell of their friend*

*enshrouded and encased in dark velvet --*

*I saw her face floating among the pink plastic roses*

*a mask that mocked the memory of her laughter*


*Where is the chime of your chatter, Bernice?*

*that giggle that would erupt in the middle of class*

*like the whoop of an angel buzzing earth...*


*How did such music end as but a memory and why?*


XLV

*You fell asleep and never awoke . . .*

*rumors of drugs feed along the bottom of conversations*

*but I don't hear those words, not now, not here,*

*and I let them burn away in the flash of  my memories of you*


*of you . . .*

*the  chatter of bells in you voice,*

*the scintillation of  joy in your eyes*

*a thousand butterflies floating on the benediction of your laughter . . .*


*How troubles ran before the assault of that brace-filled smile*

*that dispersed of gloom like dawn banishing the mist and dark*


*Youth in full bloom with all the universe before you . . .*


*Now no more*


*and I think that all things that trouble me seem so light --*

*what can I complain of in life?*

*at least I'm granted time, Bernice, where you will have no more*


*then what Bernice?*


*what of us, our lives that intercepted your meteor*

*as it flashed emerald and laughing across the banner of our benighted sky:*


*a few pictures in a yearbook, memories, this poem...*

*XLVI*

*soliloquies cast in sand*


*I ponder this*

*as I step off  into the gathering darkness*

*walking between the children playing in the yard*

*of the tiny church*

*in the neighborhood*

*there*

*below the bridge*

# Act Two

# *Etiam atque etiam:*

# *Trials of the*

# *Heart*

There is no tie deeper then love.  What age it finds you
little matters.  When it shatters so shatters your life.

The announcement cackled over the P.A. I caught the
name, jotted it down quickly on the edge of an old quiz,
coffee stained and with a galaxy of cup bottoms orbiting
its questions about Greece, and then mulled over the
parade of faces that began walking my mind. "Xochi."
Which? Was a senior now, two years ago, yes. I taught
her world history. Second seat, near the globe.

The face floated to the surface of my thoughts like a
leaf ascending the depths of a forest pond, and from the
cool darkness I witnessed again the warm eyes, heard the
lilt in the voice, and was annoyed by the incessant
combing of hair. No burdened mood, no deep melancholy.
So I thought then.

Death came graceless and clumsy into the room that day,
banging into my cabinets and desks, tripping over my
lesson plan and scattering its sheets about the class.
He finally settled into an insolent crouch in the
corner, chewing on my briefcase . . . no prince,this --
the poets and painters of the Middle Ages had got it
wrong. Just an ill-kept, reeking, insistent little
fellow with burning eyes. Monomaniac, the cutter of
souls, the one never invited to parties. He was there,
I felt him. His presence lent a morbid energy to the
kids, as always. They see it as theater, an action
movie played out in their neighborhoods. Rare for them

to realize the central truth -- when the players die on
this stage they will not be back to play again next
week.

Thespians have expiration dates on the stages of the
world.  Dark romance, dark horror, death in the minds of
the young.

The bell chimed its release; I turned to the students,
granted freedom with a wave, and watched them file out,
some somber and some chittering away -- everyone reacts
differently, always.  Lunch time and I didn't feel like
eating; so I stayed in my room to grade some papers, or
at least to stare at them for a while.

The Renaissance, an amalgamation of facts to my
students, a mosaic of ideas and dates and names jumbled
about on a dusty and cracked floor.  They had picked out
their favorites to expound on for me -- the most dreaded
part of the test, the burning incediarious circle of
death, the essay question.  The last hoop to be jumped
through before escape.  It was my hoop to jump through
now, and I took up my pen and set to work.

Galileo Galilei, some had admired the lilt of his name
and had decided to write about him.  "Leaning Tower, sun
centered theory (one had remembered the word

'heliocentric'-- amazing), the Vatican trial, and a
general bouquet of facts from his life.


I wondered sometimes what it would  be like to be famous
enough that, centuries hence, people whose language
would be a mystery to me, in places I had never known,
would be studying the events of my life.  Enough.  Lupe
had surprised me by his choice of Girolamo Savanarola
and the Bonfire of the Vanities.  Maybe he liked the
fact that he burned books as well as playing cards.  Old
Savanarola, the gad-fly of Florence, would have
condemned me in my vain day-dreams of future fame.
Ashes to ashes . . . in his case especially.


You teach and are amazed by what "knowledge" you receive
in return.  Its like playing tennis and hitting a ball
over the net and then having a bowling ball roll back.
Poetically, its like sowing handful of seeds of unknown
heritages, then waiting until germination and fruition
to discover what plants you have grown.


Ten minutes, maybe twelve . . . the mid-day Bedouins
were wandering in and staking out their usual chairs,
munching on whatever the vending machines had to
dispense that day.  I looked up and greeted each one as
he or she entered.  Jorge, Phil, Loud Lisa, Quiet Jaime,
and Benny . . . one by one, or in small chattering

cliques, they came as always -- my room, a station in the orbit of their lives.

She appeared.

She stood in the open door, at the nadir of her emotions. I recalled an image:  a Maria of Sorrows, in a medieval niche, illuminated and radiant in her agony.

I knew the cause, supposed it anyway, and I knew the liturgy that needed to be followed.  I opened the cracked bindings of the ancient text.  The rites began. I turned to the dozen students, silenced already by the apparition at the door, and directed the first act.

"Ladies and Gentlemen, would you excuse us for a few minutes, I need to talk with Linda alone, please."

Responding with the nascent maturity that impressed me anew with each occurrence, they got up, quiet, and marched out silent and somber as druids. I motioned for Linda to take a seat next to my desk and walked over to prop the class door open.  I moved to take a seat at the battleship gray hunk of metal that doubled as desk and throne to me, shuffled some papers to give myself a moment to till my words, and then began with a question whose answer I knew, like a good barrister in a trial of the heart.

"What's wrong Linda?  Share."

She went on to tell me that they had broken up two weeks ago.  She had tried to call but been rebuffed.  I let her rave, I knew enough to be patient and wait.  Hate for the world, heaven, fate, and time.  Finally, tears gained ground, silence but for the haunted sorrows that enveloped her filled the room.  My turn, I thought, and marshaled my armory of counsel.

"Life chains us with cobwebs, holds us light as a moth in its grasp -- death comes at all ages and from all causes.  I don't know why, Honey, I'm not a god.  I don't know why she had to die now.  You're right, it isn't fair, but life wins no awards for fairness . . . . You loved her, she knew it; that's what's important to think about.  Don't give death the satisfaction of taking her completely from you.  Remember.  Cherish your memories.  She will never be away.  Memories are a weapon to fight death.  They keep alive the most vital part of the people we have known -- their love for us and our love for them."

I worked what spells I could, conjured words from the

lucent regions of my heart and the shadowed avenues of
my experience, till she had to go.

The bell chimed, I offered her another tissue from the
box on my desk, and walked her to the door.  Then I
walked back to my desk and slowly sat down.  Silence.  A
moment, then two.  The first student came crashing
through the door.  Siggy.

"Hey, Dr. D., do we have a quiz today?"

"The sun rises, the sun sets, and, yes, Siggy, you have
a quiz today. It's on Martin Luther, look at the reading
from yesterday, the fifth paragraph especially, and
remind yourself why he wrote his thesis.  Oh, and also
recall the reaction of the church authorities in Rome."

It was time to close the ancient texts.  Sunset through
opaque windows, the smell of small roses rising from a
courtyard centuries old, the hush of robes brushing
cobblestones . . . I rubbed my eyes, stood up and walked
to the board and erased a few notes.  Like Linda, it was
my time to begin again . . .

# Coda:

# respice, adspice,

# prospice

In the womb of morning

past midnight

a hairbreadth beating of seconds gone

I lay awake

waiting for sleep to pass its benediction

thoughts swell and eddy

the night sounds pass gentle over me


The procession

I sense

is coming --


moving over the dark hillocks and snaking through the valley

crossing the whispering stream

whose current caresses gray round stones

dozing eternally under its chill flowing


It weaves through the maze of gnarled evergreens

moving always for the mountain castle of my thoughts

and I wait watchful for the signal

for my brain to begin its dark mass

its sacraments of wondering

ponderings and alarm


I see them approach from my pinnacle perch

looking from the gray stone battlements

like a lord witnessing the first churnings of a rebellion

I am ready

yet know not what for


By the edge of the wood

they gather up

mingle and murmur

selecting


The stars shed light

the moon rests dark in her corner of the sky

night sounds are silenced by the brooding hoard below my walls

seconds link

minutes pass

finally one soft shape emerges from the throng


how small is one in the midst of the vastness

small constellations of atoms

daunted so by the night

*He is a young man*

*black of hair*

*with curls that fall to his shoulders*

*the night is deep*

*the light scant*

*I cannot see his eyes*

*yet feel them to be blue*

*earnest and cool*

*unclouded by the dust of years*

*not yet drawn to sweep the earth with a downward gaze*


*The brave messenger walks intrepid to the stolid wall*

*stops*

*catches his words*

*and speaks*


*"Lord, what is the meaning of our days?*

*We beseech and demand an answer,*

*for how can we live without knowing why?*

*Our hearts ache for knowledge of this enigma --*

*grant us illumination, Lord, we pray thee."*


*I pause*

*look to the stars that constellation shimmer*

*diamond bouquets in the vast cathedral darkness above*

*wait for the words to be whispered into my heart*

*LVIII*

by the muse angels that seem always ready to midwife

concepts beyond my mortal keen to conceive


--Lad, the purpose lies within your breast

planted like a seed by beneficent gods.


-- Your task lies in stewardship . . .

pretend a wizened old man has handed you a seed

yet told you not what plant scioned it . . .

how would you know its true identity?


                    "By planting it in the earth, caring for it,

                              bringing it to fruition."


-- So too is it with the purpose you desire to know.


-- Learn and experience

hold open your mind to the world

keep open your heart to the murmur of nature and the divine

it time a denouement will come

your  purpose shall then be clear.


                              "But your Eminence,

                    what you say depends so on the gods;

                    yet, some in our number doubt their reality.

                              Lord , are the gods with us still?

                              Have they died as some will contend?"

*LIX*

-- *Do you breath?*

*If so*

*fear not*

*they have yet to expire . . .*


*I  hear a raven caw outside my window*

*dawn's black messenger summons*

*and from the filaments of sleep my mind escapes.*

I have had my successes, and I have suffered my
failures.  I have been in the crowd of friends when my
students celebrated the little and big festivals in
their lives.  I have celebrated with many, and  I have
stood at the gravesides of others as they were lowered
into eternity.

To get a rose to bloom in a well appointed garden is
simple, to get one to bloom in a haggard land where no
one is willing to offer you water is a task for the
strong spined.

# íte, missa est

*"The man who finds his homeland sweet*

*is still a tender beginner; he to whom every soil is as his*

*native one is already strong; but he is perfect to whom the*

*entire world is as a foreign land."*

from

Hugo of St. Victor's *Didascalicon*

*Urbi et orbi:*

Dr. Patrick Dougherty grew up in rural Michigan, in a small community, attending a peaceful set of schools surrounded by the same companions from nursery through high school. He attended college in Oregon and Austria, graduating with a B.A. in history. After college he decided to go on to graduate school and attended Northern Arizona University. It was there that he decided on his life's work of education. Teaching some college classes and working with high school students through the Bureau of Indian Affairs, he became convinced that teaching was his calling. He completed a teaching license program after finishing his MA in Modern American history.

Wanting to work with at-risk students, Pat opted for a tour of duty at a large school in south Phoenix, Arizona. His typical class consisted of students from six or seven ethnic backgrounds with a host of first languages other than English. The school population was largely Hispanic and African American, with large minorities of Asian and Native American students. The vast majority of the students were what was classically termed, "at-risk."

After ten years, two more masters degrees, a doctorate in education, two children, and a with a growing desire to have his children exposed to his wife's Japanese culture, Dr. Dougherty left Phoenix and took up a new career as a professor of English at a university in Japan. He resides in Himeji, Japan, living in an old section of the city, within view of its ancient samurai castle. Pat, when asked about his teaching experiences, always cites his time in Phoenix as the crucible in which his talents were fired and tempered. "Those were tough, beautiful, and fulfilling years," he says. "You couldn't just get by in that situation, you had to grasp these kids' attentions, steal their thoughts away from the chaos that so many of them had to deal with in their personal lives. You learned to be an actor, steward, guide, counselor, father confessor, curriculum expert, and master communicator. If you could maintain your sanity, the environment was thrilling in a way that extreme sports cannot duplicate," explained Pat.

Printed in the United States
By Bookmasters